Brian Wildsmith

DAISY

PANTHEON BOOKS   NEW YORK

Farmer Brown was a very hard worker. Every day he worked in his fields until the sun went down. After his dinner he liked to watch television. One night he saw an advertisement for a shiny new tractor. "I'd love to have a machine like that," he thought. "It would make my life much easier."

One day on his way home, Farmer Brown forgot to close the gate to Daisy's field.

"Now is m__ as she dash__ He was so tired he didn't even watch television. He ate a small supper and then went straight to bed.

But when she came to the edge of a roof, she was frightened and didn't know what to do. "Look at the cow on the roof," shouted the villagers. "How can we get her down?"

"That looks like Daisy," said the village priest. "Call Farmer Brown. He'll know what to do."

The next day Farmer Brown bought a shiny new tractor. The producer took Daisy to a nearby port. There she was hoisted aboard a ship and taken to Hollywood. "Now I will really see the world," thought Daisy.

In Hollywood everyone loved
Daisy.

DAISY
COW
OF THE
YEAR

She even appeared in a bubble-
bath advertisement.

And great banquets were held in her honor. She was served all kinds of delicious food . . .

"This is not proper food for a cow to eat." And she kicked all her food onto the floor.

Daisy began to grow thin. She became pale and sad, and the producer was very worried about her health. He took her to see a famous veterinarian.

The producer was a kind man, and he had grown very fond of Daisy. It upset him to see her so sad. "All right, Daisy," he said, "we'll make one last movie. And it will be the most spectacular one of all."

The movie was called *Daisy Come Home*. In the last scene Daisy was flown on an airplane high in the sky.

Daisy mooed with joy as she floated gently down through the air, going home.
She was overjoyed to be in her own field and to smell the grass and buttercups again. Just then Farmer Brown drove up in his shiny new tractor.
"It's wonderful to have you back," he said, throwing his arms around Daisy. "This field didn't seem the same without you. I've missed you!"

Together they went home. In the
evenings they both watched
television. Farmer Brown
wasn't so tired now that
he had his tractor.

For my Mother
and my Father

Library of Congress Cataloging in Publication Data
Wildsmith, Brian. Daisy.
Summary: A cow's dream of seeing the world comes true,
but it doesn't bring her happiness.
[1. Cows—Fiction]   I. Title.
PZ7.W647.Dai   1984   [E]   83-12150
ISBN 0-394-85975-8
ISBN 0-394-95975-2 (lib. bdg.)